"This charming and realistic book helps children learn to talk about their feelings rather than act out. Charlie has big feelings about adoption, identity and birth parents and acts out his feelings. He is helped by his adopted mother to express his feelings in a positive way including an art project. The children I have used this book with love him and love doing the project."

—*Regina M. Kupecky, social worker at The Attachment and Bonding Center of Ohio, co-author of* Adopting the Hurt Child, Parenting the Hurt Child, A Foster-Adoption Story: Angela and Michael's Journey *and* The Case of the Multiple Mothers

"I consider *A Place in My Heart* one of the very best books for young adopted children (and their parents) because it demonstrates how to make it 'OK' for children to hold their feelings and connections for both of their 'real' families: their birth parents and their adoptive parents. No surprise the book was written by an adult adoptee—she really 'gets it'!"

—*Beth Hall, Director, Pact: An Adoption Alliance www.pactadopt.org, author of* Inside Transracial Adoption

of related interest

Forever Fingerprints
An Amazing Discovery for Adopted Children
Sherrie Eldridge
ISBN 978 1 84905 778 3
eIBSN 978 1 78450 021 4

Adopted Like Me
My Book of Adopted Heroes
Ann Angel
ISBN 978 1 84905 935 0
eISBN 978 0 85700 740 7

Can I tell you about Adoption?
A guide for friends, family and professionals
Anne Braff Brodzinsky
ISBN 978 1 84905 942 8
eISBN 978 0 85700 759 9

The Mulberry Bird
An Adoption Story
Anne Braff Brodzinsky
ISBN 978 1 84905 933 6
eISBN 978 0 85700 720 9

How Are You Feeling Today Baby Bear?
Exploring Big Feelings After Living in a Stormy Home
Jane Evans
ISBN 978 1 84905 424 9
eISBN 978 0 85700 793 3

A Safe Place for Caleb
An Interactive Book for Kids, Teens and Adults
with Issues of Attachment, Grief, Loss or Early Trauma
Kathleen A. Chara and Paul J. Chara, Jr.
ISBN 978 1 84310 799 6
eISBN 978 1 84642 143 3

MARY GROSSNICKLE

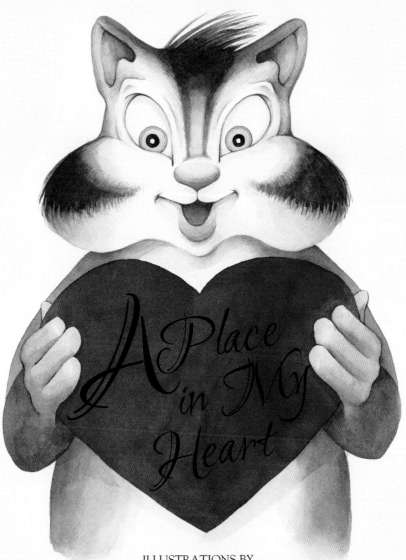

A Place in My Heart

ILLUSTRATIONS BY
ALISON RELYEA-PARR

Jessica Kingsley *Publishers*
London and Philadelphia

First published in 2004 by Speaking of Adoption

This edition published in 2014
by Jessica Kingsley Publishers
73 Collier Street
London N1 9BE, UK
and
400 Market Street, Suite 400 Philadelphia,
PA 19106, USA

www.jkp.com

Library of Congress Cataloging in Publication Data
Grossnickle, Mary.
A place in my heart / Mary Grossnickle ; illustrated by Alison Relyea.
    pages cm
"First published in 2004 by Speaking of Adoption."
Summary: Charlie, a chipmunk adopted by a family of squirrels, begins to wonder about his
birthparents but is afraid that asking questions will upset his family.
ISBN 978-1-84905-771-4 (alk. paper)
[1. Adoption--Fiction. 2. Birthparents--Fiction. 3. Family life--Fiction. 4. Chipmunks--Fiction. 5. Squirrels--Fiction.]
I. Relyea, Alison illustrator. II. Title.
 PZ7.G90875Pl 2014
 [E]--dc23
                    2014011070

British Library Cataloguing in Publication Data
A CIP catalogue record for this book is available from the British Library

 ISBN 978 1 84905 771 4
 eISBN 978 1 78450 022 1

Printed and bound in China

Dedication

 To all my parents

As soon as the sun came up each morning,
Charlie bolted out the door of his house
and headed for the woods.

He couldn't wait to get out and run!

"Whee!"
Charlie cried as he sailed over a dead log.

He darted under piles of brush and
sprinted between rocks and through mounds of leaves.

As he ran, Charlie happily sang,
"Chip! Chip! Chip!"

After his morning run, Charlie found an oak tree
with plenty of plump acorns.
When he packed the acorns into his mouth,
his cheeks were as big as his whole head!

With his cheeks full of acorns,
he raced home to share the food with
his mother and father and his brother and two sisters.

"Chip! Chip! Chip!" Charlie cheerfully called.
They all came running and gathered around the pile of acorns.

"This is yummy," Charlie's brother said as he gobbled his breakfast.
"For a little guy, you sure bring home a lot of food!"

"A little guy,"
Charlie thought crossly as he munched a big acorn.
"I'm always the littlest."

It was true.
Charlie was the smallest
member of the family.

He was short and brown, and he had
black and white stripes down his back.
His tail was thin and furry.

His mother and father
and brother and sisters were
taller and chubbier than Charlie.

Everyone except Charlie was gray,
with no stripes at all,
and their tails were big and bushy.

That night when Charlie's mother
was tucking him into bed, Charlie asked,
"Mommy, why don't I look like you and Daddy?"
Charlie already knew the answer,
but he liked to hear his mother tell the story.

Charlie's mother said,
"Well, you grew inside a different mother's tummy.
She is called your birthmother. And you have a birthfather, too.
You probably look like they do."

"Why don't I live with them?" Charlie asked.

"Your birthmother and birthfather weren't ready
to be a mommy and daddy when you were little,"
Charlie's mother replied.
"And we wanted another child.
You came to live with us, and that made us very happy!"

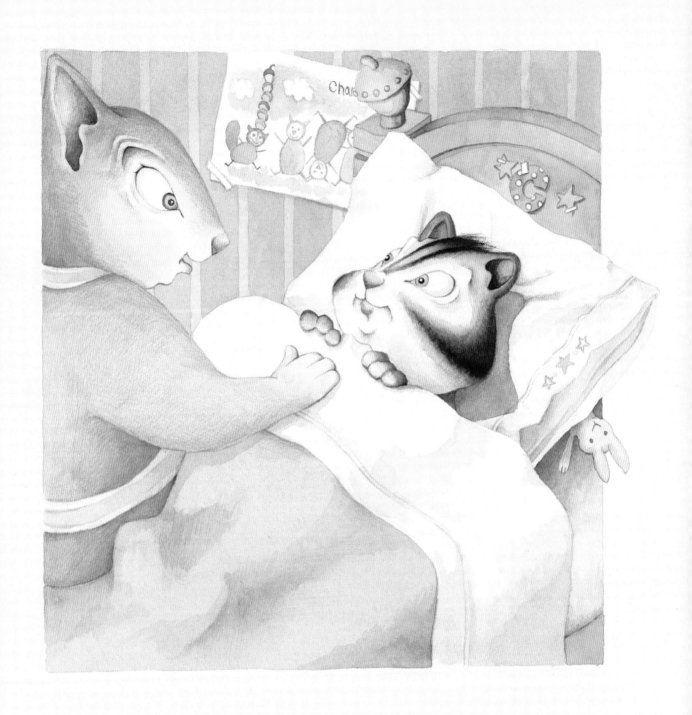

Charlie smiled.
He loved to hear about how he joined his family.

Suddenly he wrinkled his brow
and asked,
"Does that mean I have two mothers and two fathers?"

"Well," his mother answered,
"you have a birthmother and birthfather who made you.
And you have a forever Mother and forever Father."

"I know who that is!" Charlie exclaimed.
"That's you and Daddy!
You are my forever Mommy and forever Daddy."

"That's right, Charlie.
We are your forever family."
His mother smiled as she gave him a big hug.

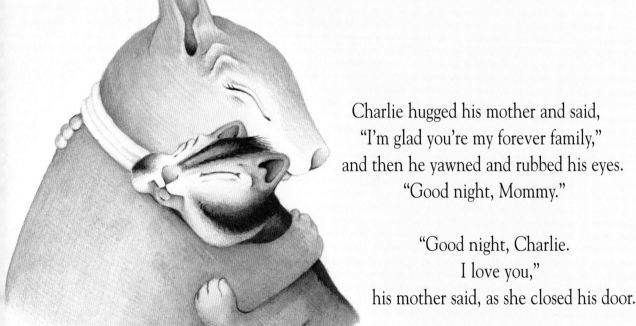

Charlie hugged his mother and said,
"I'm glad you're my forever family,"
and then he yawned and rubbed his eyes.
"Good night, Mommy."

"Good night, Charlie.
I love you,"
his mother said, as she closed his door.

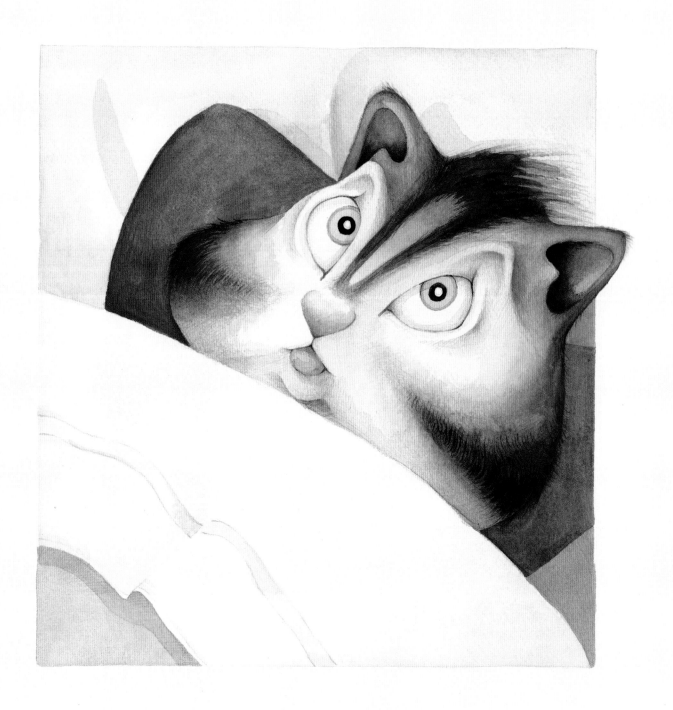

"I love you too, Mommy," Charlie said quietly.
But Charlie couldn't fall asleep.

He folded his arms behind his head and thought for a long time.

The next day Charlie didn't feel like running.

He didn't sing,
"Chip! Chip! Chip!"

And he didn't gather acorns for breakfast.

Instead, he walked slowly
to his thinking place,
an old hollow log at the edge of the woods.

He laid his head on his little brown paws and peered out.
Charlie had a lot to think about.

He had a birthmother and a birthfather.
And he had a forever Mommy and a forever Daddy.

"I know what Mommy and Daddy look like," Charlie thought.

"But I wonder what my birthmother and birthfather look like.
Do I look like them?"

Charlie stayed in his thinking place
almost all morning
and thought
about his birthmother and birthfather.

"I wonder what their names are,"
Charlie murmured.

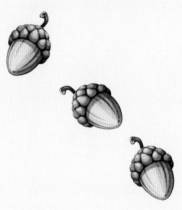

Turning over on his back, Charlie watched the clouds.

"I bet my birthmother is beautiful,"
he sighed.

"Maybe my birthfather
is famous.
He could be a sports star!"

When his brother and sisters
begged him to come and play,
Charlie finally scampered out to join them.

But instead of playing,
he bit his brother on the nose.
He teased his sisters and pulled their tails.

No one was having much fun,
and they were glad when they heard their mother call,
"Lunchtime!"

During lunch,
Charlie played with his food.
He forgot to say please and thank you.

He didn't use his napkin,
and he spilled his milk.

And his mother had to ask him
three times
to keep his elbows off the table.

Charlie's mother knew
that something was troubling him.
After lunch, she sat down in her favorite chair
and pulled him onto her lap.

"Charlie, honey," she said,
"I think you're having a tough day today.
Sometimes you look mad, and sometimes you look sad."

Charlie curled into a little ball on his mother's lap.
He didn't know what to say.

"Last night we talked about
your birthmother and birthfather,"
she softly continued,
"and I wonder
if you've been thinking about them."

Charlie looked up at his mother.

"Well, maybe,"

Charlie said in a voice so quiet it was almost a whisper.

"It's OK to think about your birthmother and birthfather,"
Charlie's mother said.

Charlie snuggled in his mother's arms.
Then he said in a quiet little voice,
"I wonder
if they think about me."

"I'm sure they think about you, Charlie,"
his mother replied as she kissed the top of his head.
"You have a very special place in their hearts."

"Maybe
they don't have room in their hearts for me,"
Charlie said sadly.

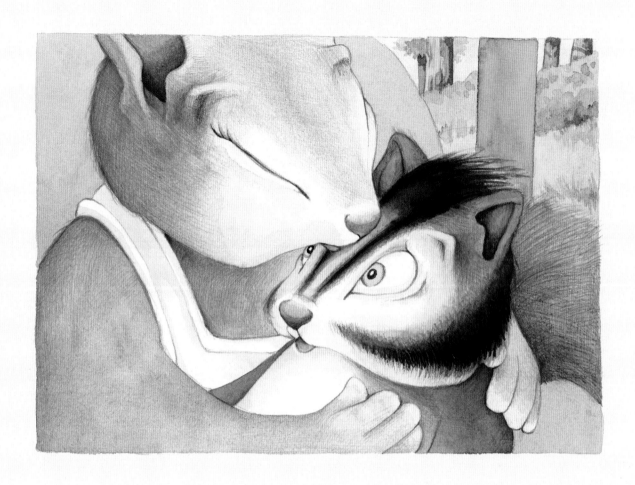

"We have room in our hearts
for everybody we care about, Charlie,"
his mother said wisely.

"I'll show you what I mean."

Charlie's mother found two very large pieces of red paper.
She cut each piece into a giant heart.

"This is your heart," she explained, handing Charlie one of the hearts.
"And this is my heart."

"I'm going to write the names of everyone I keep in my heart,"
Charlie's mother said as she started to write.

Soon her heart was so full that she had
to write some names on top of other names!
Charlie tried to count the names,
but there were too many.

"Now it's your turn, Charlie.
Who has a place in your heart?" she asked.

Charlie said, "You and Daddy."
He wrote Mommy and Daddy in very big letters in the middle of the heart.

"And my brother and sisters," Charlie said.
He concentrated and wrote Abby and Libby and Max.

Charlie wrote Grandma and Grandpa, then Aunt Sophie and Uncle Chester.
He wrote the names of all his cousins and all his friends.

Finally he set down his pencil.
"Whew!
I think I'm done," he said.

"Look at all the people we care about, Charlie," his mother said.
"And they care about us, too.
Isn't it wonderful?"

Charlie's mother looked at him tenderly and asked,
"Is there anyone else you'd like to add?
Maybe someone you've been thinking about lately?"

Charlie sat and stared at his red paper heart.

"Well," Charlie finally said,
"I have my birthmother and my birthfather."

"But I don't think about them all the time. I just *wonder* about them sometimes.
Besides, my heart is pretty full already."

"The best thing about hearts, Charlie," his mother said,
"is that they can never be too full."

"I'm not sure, Mommy," Charlie said.
"I don't want to make
you and Daddy sad by giving my
birthmother and birthfather a
place in my heart."

"Oh, Sweetie," said Charlie's mother.
"That wouldn't make us sad."

Charlie hesitated.
"Are you sure, Mommy?"

"Yes," his mother answered gently, "I'm very sure."

"OK, Mommy," he said as he wrote.
"Then I'd like to give my
birthmother and birthfather a place in my heart."

After he finished writing, he looked up at his mother.

When he saw her smiling,
Charlie's face broke into a huge grin.

Through the open window came the sounds of a wild game of tag.

Charlie heard someone yell,
"Charlie, come and play!"

Charlie jumped up.
His eyes sparkled, and he gave his mother a quick hug.

"I'm going outside now, Mommy,"
Charlie called
as he dashed toward the door.
"I love you a whole bunch, Mommy. Bye!"

And he scampered off singing,
"Chip! Chip! Chip!"

Mary Grossnickle was adopted as a toddler.
She provides post-adoption information and
support to adoptive families in Wisconsin,
where she lives on a lake and is visited frequently
by chipmunks and squirrels.

Alison Relyea-Parr lives in Wisconsin
with her husband, two daughters, and
three tabby cats.
Visit her at alisonrelyea.com